D0708328

3 0116 02015079 1

For Evlynn,
with love, Lauren

For Louie,
love Polly

PUFFIN BOOKS
Published by the Penguin Group: London, New York, Australia,
Canada, India, Ireland, New Zealand and South Africa
Penguin Books Ltd, Registered Offices: 80 Strand, London WC2R 0RL, England

puffinbooks.com

First published 2005
This edition published 2014
001
Thank you to Tony Clark for taking the photo of Louie Moe Hillcoat
Text, illustration and stage design copyright © Lauren Child, 2005
Photographs copyright © Polly Borland, 2005
Made and printed in Slovakia
ISBN: 978–0–141–34366–2

The Princess and the Pea

IN MINIATURE

AFTER THE FAIRY TALE BY
HANS CHRISTIAN ANDERSEN

LAUREN CHILD

CAPTURED BY POLLY BORLAND

PUFFIN

**NCE UPON A**
time, many *moons*
ago, *of course*, there
was a king and a
queen who had a
prince for a son.
He was a nice boy and not unpleasant
to look at – in fact, handsome –
not *too* handsome,
just handsome
enough.

NE DAY WHEN THE PRINCE
was old enough, his parents decided it was time
for him to be married. *You know what parents
are like and a prince's parents are no different.*

The prince didn't object to the idea but he
did make one condition –

he wanted to marry for *love*.

He was just that kind of romantic *boy.*

He told his father and his mother, 'I would gladly marry tomorrow but, whoever
she is, she must be **more** *mesmerising* **than the** *moon* and I must
find her **more** *fascinating* **than all the** *stars* **in the sky.**
And there must be a certain...something about her.'

'What *something*?' asked the queen.
'Just ... *something*,' replied the prince.

'Yes, yes,' agreed the king, 'that's all very lovely but our condition is that
she must be a **princess** of blue blood and equal in royalness to you.'
The prince wasn't all that interested in these details but knew he wouldn't
get any peace until he agreed.

So he did.

*Now, you may think finding yourself a suitable princess would be easy to do if you
are a handsome prince but you would be wrong – just how many* mesmerising
and fascinating *princesses do you imagine there are out there?*

Well, the king and queen did all the traditional fairy-tale things in order that
their son might be bowled over by the right girl.

*T*HEY threw a
Royal Ball and invited
all the single royal
girls in the land.

Everyone
said *yes*.

Everyone
danced.

Everyone
had a good time.

But none of them
captured
the prince's
heart.

THE PRINCE EXPLAINED TO THE king and the queen how simply *none* of them was *mesmerising* or *fascinating*. And *none* of them, *not one* of them, had a *certain... something* about them. No, if he couldn't marry for love, then he would rather live alone for all eternity, gazing at **all the stars in the night sky.** *Not only was he romantic but also a little dramatic.*

The king and the queen said, 'The thing is, our dear son, what you are really looking for is a *real* **princess**, and a *real* **princess** is a rare thing indeed.'

'They do not grow on trees,' said the king.

'No, no, they do not,' said the queen.

'You see,' said the king, 'a *real* **princess** is not only *mesmerisingly* beautiful and *fascinatingly* interesting but, most important of all –'

'She has **manners**,' said the queen.

'No one should ever travel without them,' said the king.

'No, never, never go anywhere without your **manners**,' agreed the queen, taking her elbows off the table.

'The only problem with *real* **princesses**,' sighed the king, 'is that they are terribly hard to get hold of and they almost never read their post.'

'No indeed,' said the queen, '*real* **princesses** are very hard to come by. No one has ever found one by looking, you just have to wait for one to come to you.'

UT THE PRINCE,
who rarely listened to his mother's advice, did the traditional fairy-tale find-yourself-a-bride thing of riding **far** and **wide** looking throughout the kingdom for a *real* princess.

He even rode
far and **wide**
to other people's
kingdoms.

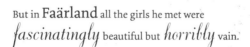

But in Faärland all the girls he met were *fascinatingly* beautiful but *horribly* vain.

*A*ND in the kingdom of **Schonan** they were all
mesmerisingly clever but *exceedingly* dull.

*A*ND in Harvonia there was a *certain*...
   silliness about them. I mean, you can see his problem, can't you?

$\mathcal{T}$HE prince
came back very
downcast. He
refused to
eat anything
for supper,
not even the
very delicious
rook pie the
royal cook had
prepared as a
welcome home.

He lit a
candle
in his
window
and just
stood and
gazed
into the
night sky.

$\mathcal{N}$OT so
far away, in a
treetop house
just over the
mountain, there
was a girl with
the most beautiful
black, black
hair you have ever
seen, *or possibly
never seen.*

She woke up that
night to see the
moon dancing
on her ceiling,
and she popped
on her favourite
pea-green
dress and glided
down the stairs
into the garden.

*T*HE moonlight
shone in such a
magical way
that she wondered
to herself if it could
possibly look as
beautiful on
the other side of
the garden wall.
So she tripped down
the garden path,
stepped over a pile of
unopened letters
and slipped
through the gate,
where she saw
the *moon*
perched on top
of the mountain.

'I wonder if the
moon would be
as *beautiful* up
there,' she thought
out loud.

*A*ND it was,
so she continued
walking, right down
the other side of
the mountain until
she came to the
wild woods.

'Would it be so
beautiful in
the woods?'
considered the girl.

And **it was**,

it really was.

But just as she came
out of the woods a
dark *cloud* moved
across the *moon*
and **suddenly**…

it wasn't.

**OTHER, THOUGHT THE GIRL.**
She could feel a heavy storm brewing. She would
never make it back to her own little tree house in
time. There was nothing for it but to walk on.

So on she walked.

She had not gone more than *seven* steps when
she felt the first heavy drop of rain fall on her cheek.

Bother, thought the girl. Within *three* minutes she was already
soaked to the skin, and her *two* shoes were filling with water.

The *wind* was **howling**,
the *trees* were **creaking** and **cracking** as if they might part
company with their roots, and the *rain* **pounded** down and
the *lightning* flashed its forked tongue in the blackened sky.
And the girl began to tire.
It was not umbrella weather, no, an umbrella would have done you no good at all.

❦

'Hmmm, I think I might just catch a *terrible* cold, unless I have the very
good fortune to spot a light in a window . . . but what is the likelihood of that on
this **wild, wild** night in the middle of *nowhere*?' said the girl out loud.

However, as she made her way round the next corner, that's **exactly** what
she saw. Using her very last drop of energy
she climbed the **steep, steep** steps
to the **huge** front door.

$\mathcal{T}$HE queen was woken all of a sudden by a very, very loud knock at the palace door. Being a queen she sensibly woke her husband, an unusually heavy sleeper, and asked him to 'go and see who in all the kingdom might be banging on the door at this time of night, for goodness' sake.'

WHEN the king opened the door, what he saw was a dripping wet girl standing *(without even a coat)* on his doorstep. She had long raven-black hair and skin as **pale** as ivory and lips as red as rose petals. *You know how it is with these fairy-tale types.* She was, despite the effects of the weather, a *real* beauty. But she was also shivering cold and looked as if she might collapse at any moment.

Of course, the king was very polite. *He had manners. That's the thing about real kings, their manners are impeccable.* He didn't even mention the large puddle that was forming on his very expensive royal floor.

Instead

he told the girl
to warm herself
by the fire
while he called
for his wife.

*Who didn't
particularly
want to get up
on such an
unreasonable
night, but being
a real queen
never ever
forgot to be
hospitable
to strangers.*

HE QUEEN THOUGHT
this girl looked special, there was
something *mesmerising*,
something *fascinating*,
something . . . *something*
that the queen could not quite put her finger on.

Unlike her husband she came straight to
the point. 'So, my dear, who are you on such a wild and unruly night?'

'Oh, I am a princess and I live in a tree house on the other side
of the mountain.'

'A *tree house*?' pondered the king.

'A *princess*,' enquired the queen. 'What kind of princess?'

'Oh, I –' replied the girl, 'I am a *real* princess. I was outside admiring
the *moon* when it started to *rain* and then, what with the *thunder*
and *lightning*, well, then I lost my way and then I saw a light in your window . . .
I do hope you can forgive my waking you at such an hour.'

The queen thought, Well, she **sounds** like a *real* princess,
she **looks** like a *real* princess, but we'll see.

So after the girl had finished her elderflower cordial, the queen ordered
a steaming hot bath and supplied her with the softest towels and an
exquisite nightgown.

'Oh, this is far too good for me,' said the girl, *which, of course, is
exactly the kind of thing a* real *princess would say.*

*W*HILE the girl was taking her bath, the queen had the servants make up the bed – in a most unusual fashion.

She chose the most fabulous bedchamber with the most *beautiful* four-poster bed. Then right in the middle of the bed she placed a tiny, tiny **pea-green** *pea* from the royal garden, then on top of the *pea* she piled one, two, three, four, five, six, seven, eight, nine, ten, eleven, twelve feather mattresses. And on top of the **twelve** mattresses she placed the *finest* linen sheets and the plumpest Siberian goose-down pillows.

'WHAT a beautiful bed,' gasped the girl. 'Oh, I am sure I will sleep
like a *real* **princess** in this bed.' And up the ladder she climbed.
We'll see, thought the queen.

*B*UT that night the poor girl hardly slept a wink. She was tossing and turning all night. Despite her exhaustion she could not make herself comfortable. Worse still, the next morning she found she was black and blue and rather achy.

T DAYBREAK THE QUEEN
knocked on the door with a cup of tea.
'How did you sleep, my dear?
I trust comfortably.'

Not wanting to be rude, the girl
replied, 'Oh, very well. Yes, perfectly.
Thank you so much for asking.'

Aha, thought the queen, I knew
she couldn't really be a *real, real* **princess**.

*But what the queen was forgetting was that any real princess
has such impeccable manners that it would be impossible for her
to tell her host, who had gone to all the effort of making her a bed
stacked with twelve feather mattresses, that, in fact, it was the
most uncomfortable night that she had ever had, in all her life.*

The queen, though most disappointed, invited her young guest
to have breakfast down in the royal dining room.

WHEN the prince saw the girl his eyes lit up.

He thought she was **more** *mesmerising* **than the** *moon* and when she spoke he found her **more** *fascinating* **than the** *stars.*

And there was a *certain…* *something* about her that caused him to let go of his teacup, which clattered to the floor.

**HE PRINCESS COULDN'T**
help thinking there was

something *romantic,*
something *dramatic,*
something . . . *strangely charming*

about his clumsiness, and she bent down to pick up
the cup. A *real princess* *will always pick up your teacup if you drop it – kindness*
is practically their middle name – but this was not the only reason she did so.

There was a light in the prince's dark eyes which reminded her of

all the *stars* in the night sky.

It did not escape the queen's notice that as the girl bent down she let out a cry
something a bit like *ouch.*

'Whatever is the matter, my dear?' asked the king.

'Oh dear, I am all aches and pains today and I just don't know why and I feel
so awful when you went to so much effort and how ungrateful I must seem and
I hope you will forgive me.'

But there was nothing to forgive because, as anyone will know, a girl who
can turn black and blue when a tiny, tiny pea-green garden *pea* is placed
under twelve feather mattresses, must just surely be a *real* princess.

The prince, who was not very bothered about this detail, simply said,

'There's a *certain something* about you.'

And the girl smiled and told him her name.

AND after the
m**ᴏᴏ**n had risen
and set several more
times, the prince
asked the girl to
marry him.
That's the thing about
real princes,
they know all the right
questions to ask.

And she being a
bright girl – *as all*
real **princesses**
are – knew a
real **prince**
when she saw one,
and said *yes.*

And they were
married in a very
real fashion,
outside in a garden
where the sky
twinkled with *stars*
and the m**ᴏᴏ**n
shone down and
everyone had
a splendid time.

$\mathcal{P}$EAS
were not served because,
as everyone knows,
real princesses
are not especially fond of
peas.

Lauren Child is one of today's most talented and innovative children's writers and illustrators. Winner of the *Smarties Prize* and the *Kate Greenaway Medal*, Lauren is best known for her *Clarice Bean* and *Charlie and Lola* books. Charlie and Lola now feature in the wonderful animated television series.

Polly Borland is an internationally acclaimed portrait photographer, whose commissions include the Queen, Germaine Greer and Nick Cave. She has won the *John Kobal Portrait Award* and is a fellow of the Royal Photographic Society. She has exhibited at the National Portrait Gallery in London as well as in her native Australia.

In this book Lauren has collaborated with Polly, to set *The Princess and the Pea* in a miniature, 3-dimensional world. The joy for Lauren of working with a photographer like Polly was the ability to capture a moment – so you can almost imagine the characters have just walked into the room.

'I love the paintings of Vermeer, his detail and the way he allows you a glimpse into someone else's world' – LAUREN

'Lauren had a very clear idea of how she wanted each scene to look. As the photographer my job was to breathe life into them' – POLLY